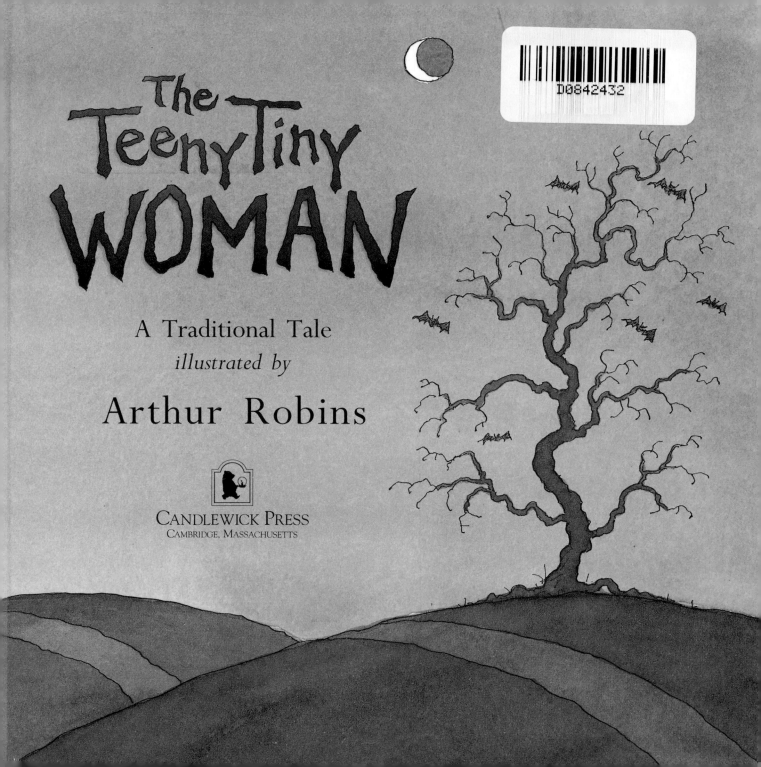

The TeenyTiny WOMAN

A Traditional Tale

illustrated by

Arthur Robins

CANDLEWICK PRESS
CAMBRIDGE, MASSACHUSETTS

Once upon a time

a teeny tiny woman

who lived in a teeny tiny house

put on her teeny tiny hat

and went out for a teeny tiny walk.

When the teeny tiny woman

had gone a teeny tiny way,

she went through a teeny tiny gate

into a teeny tiny churchyard.

In the teeny tiny churchyard

the teeny tiny woman

found a teeny tiny bone

on a teeny tiny grave.

Then the teeny tiny woman

said to her teeny tiny self,

"This teeny tiny bone

will make some teeny tiny soup

for my teeny tiny supper."

So the teeny tiny woman

took the teeny tiny bone

back to her teeny tiny house.

When she got home

she felt a teeny tiny tired,

so she put the teeny tiny bone

in her teeny tiny cupboard

and got into her teeny tiny bed

for a teeny tiny sleep.

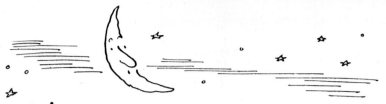

After a teeny tiny while

the teeny tiny woman

was woken by a teeny tiny voice

that said,

"Give me my bone!"

The teeny tiny woman

was a teeny tiny frightened,

so she hid her teeny tiny head

under her teeny tiny sheet.

Then the teeny tiny voice

said a teeny tiny closer

and a teeny tiny louder,

"Give me my bone!"

This made the teeny tiny woman

a teeny tiny more frightened,

so she hid her teeny tiny head

a teeny tiny farther

under her teeny tiny sheet.

Then the teeny tiny voice

said a teeny tiny closer

and a teeny tiny louder,

"Give me my bone!"

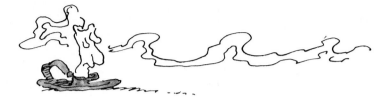

The teeny tiny woman

was a teeny tiny more frightened,

but she put her teeny tiny head

out from under her teeny tiny sheet

and said in her loudest teeny tiny voice,

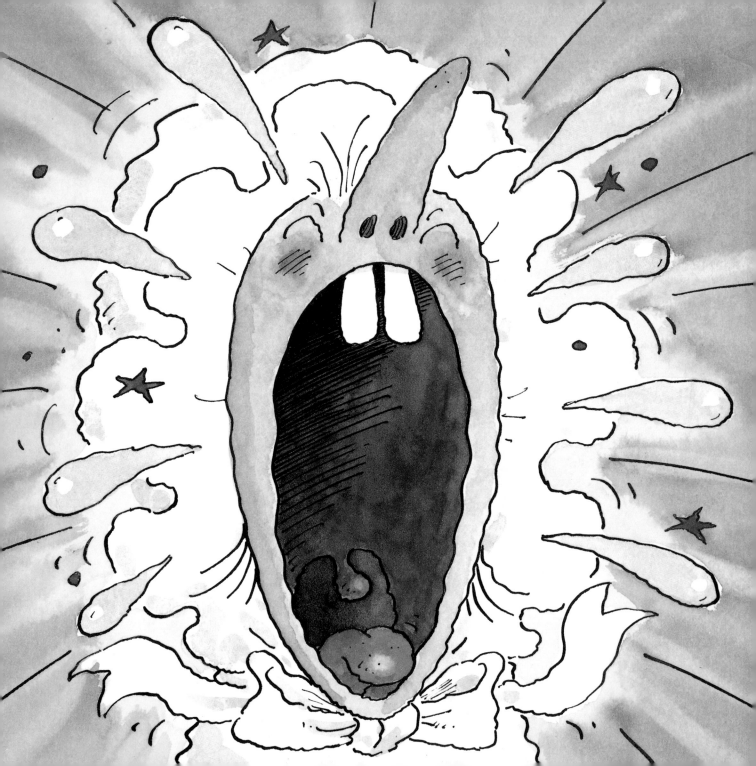

For Deirdre

First U.S. edition 1998

Library of Congress Cataloging-in-Publication Data

Robins, Arthur.
The teeny tiny woman / retold and illustrated by Arthur Robins.
—1st U.S. ed.
p.   cm.
Summary: A teeny tiny woman finds a teeny tiny bone in a churchyard
and puts it away in her cupboard before she goes to sleep, only to be
awakened by a teeny tiny voice demanding the return of the bone.
ISBN 0-7636-0444-5 (hardcover).—ISBN 0-7636-0452-6 (paperback)
[1. Folklore—England.]   I. Title.
PZ8.1.R555Te   1998   398.2'0942'02—dc21   [E]—97-32302

10 9 8 7 6 5 4 3 2 1

Printed in Singapore

This book was typeset in M Perpetua.
The pictures were done in pen and watercolor.

Candlewick Press
2067 Massachusetts Avenue
Cambridge, Massachusetts 02140